Leo, You Are a Star!

Story by Jackie Tidey

Illustrated by Craig Smith

Chapter 1

The Missing Sneaker

Paddy was looking under his bed for something.

There were lots of things under Paddy's bed!

3

"Paddy, it's late. Please hurry up.
You are going to miss the bus," said Mom.
"Remember, it's the school picnic today.
I have packed a picnic lunch for you."

4

"I'm almost dressed, Mom," said Paddy,
sliding out from under the bed.
"I just can't find my other sneaker."

"Leo, do you know where my sneaker is?"
Paddy said to his dog.

Leo put his head to one side
and looked at Paddy.

"Never mind, Leo.
Come on, let's get some breakfast," he said.

Chapter 2
Looking Everywhere

Paddy and Leo went into the kitchen.

"Did you find your sneaker, Paddy?" asked Mom.

Paddy shook his head and lifted his leg so Mom could see.

"Well, you can't go to school
with one sneaker on," said Mom.
"You will have to put on your old sneakers,
Paddy," she said.

"Oh, Mom," said Paddy.
"My old sneakers smell."

Mom looked at the clock.
"Well, you have five minutes
to find the other sneaker," she said.
"The bus comes at eight o'clock.
Off you go."

"Come on, Leo," said Paddy.
"You can help me find it."

Paddy and Leo ran into the TV room.
Paddy looked under the cushions on the chair.
Leo stood on his back legs and looked, too.

Paddy looked under the beanbag
in front of the TV.
Leo sniffed around the beanbag.

Paddy looked under the rug.
Leo ran under the rug and sniffed around.

"Leo, I must find my other sneaker,"
said Paddy.
"I'm going to miss the school bus . . .
and the school picnic!"

Leo ran out of the TV room.

Chapter 3

Leo's Surprise

Paddy went back into the kitchen.

Mom looked up at the clock again.
"Paddy, please go and get your old sneakers,"
she said.
"If you miss the bus, you won't get to school."

Paddy opened the back door
to get his old sneakers
from the box outside.

Leo ran inside with something in his mouth.

"Look, Paddy! Leo has a surprise for you,"
said Mom.

Leo put the missing sneaker at Paddy's feet.

"Leo, you are a star!" Paddy said,
as he quickly put on the other sneaker.

"And you are a lucky boy
to have a clever dog like Leo," said Mom.

"I know, Mom. I know," laughed Paddy.
"Leo's a cool dog!"

Paddy took his lunch from Mom
and ran to get the bus.